FIONA'S LITTLE ACCIDENT

ROSEMARY WELLS

WALKER BOOKS
AND SUBSIDIARIES

LONDON · BOSTON · SYDNEY · AUCKLAND

Fiona and her best friend, Felix, had built a volcano.

It was going to erupt big-time at show-and-tell.

At bedtime Fiona laid out her aloha dress,
her sunshine undies, and her new red shoes.

In the morning, Fiona was all volcano talk.

"The sea will boil and the sky will go dark!" said Fiona.

"Did you use the bathroom, dear?" asked Fiona's mama.

"Yes, yes, Mama!" answered Fiona.

"Are you sure?" asked Fiona's mama.

"Sure as sure is sure!" said Fiona.

This was not really true.

On the school bus Fiona told herself, *I'll have plenty of time to run to the bathoom at school when the bus pulls in.* But the bus was late.

Up staggered Felix with Mount Vesuvius on his head.
Bing-bing-bing-bing-bing! the school bell rang.
There was no time for Fiona to go to the bathroom.

In the back of Miss B's class, Felix and Fiona
readied their volcano. Then they waited for
Miss B to call on them.

But Miss B called on Victor first.

Victor brought his trick goldfish for show-and-tell.

Victor and his goldfish took for ever.

Next Miss B called on Bethany.

Bethany played "Hawaiian Holiday" on her ukulele.

Fiona waved her hand to go to the bathroom.

But the bathroom was busy.

"Come out! Come out!" whispered Fiona.

But whoever was in there was very busy.

"Volcano time!" called Miss B.

Carefully, Fiona poured instant lava into the crater.

Felix added the activator fluid.

KA-BLAM! The lava erupted with a giant belch.
It gushed upwards, spewing a spectacular cloud of glitter.
At that very moment, Fiona's accident happened.

Everyone saw Fiona have the accident.
Fiona knew everyone saw.
She wanted never, ever to be seen again.

Fiona tossed her sunshine undies in the dustbin and sped to the Harmony Corner.

There she dived deep behind the relaxation beanbags.

Felix found her.

"I'll never come out!" declared Fiona. "Ever!"

"Don't worry," said Felix. "Accidents have happened to everyone in the world! Even kings. Even queens!"

"The whole class will laugh at me for fifty years!"
said Fiona.

"They won't remember it for fifty seconds,"
said Felix.

Inch by inch, Fiona came out from her hiding place.

"Welcome back, Fiona!" said Miss B.

On Miss B's lap was a pair of clean, dry bluebell undies in a zip bag. "Your mama brought these to school for you," said Miss B.

Fiona put the bluebell undies on.

Bravely, Fiona went back to class.

Not one classmate paid any attention to Fiona.

The reason was that Victor had just made his goldfish jump into his mouth.

"He swallowed it!" yelled Humphrey.

Before Miss B could call the school nurse,
Victor yelled, "Out!"

Out jumped the goldfish back into its bowl.

The whole class chattered about Victor almost
swallowing his goldfish for the rest of the day.

"Nobody seems to remember about my accident
at all!" said Fiona.

"I told you," said Felix. "It took them fifty seconds to forget it!"

"Forty nine and a half seconds!" said Fiona.

1. Open volcano kit.

2. Place lava bowl inside frame.

5. Tear newspaper into strips and mix with paste in a bowl.

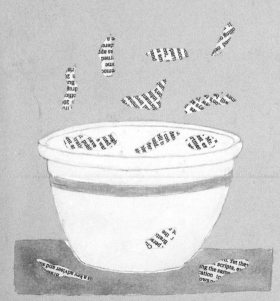

6. Smooth onto wire cone. Let dry completely.

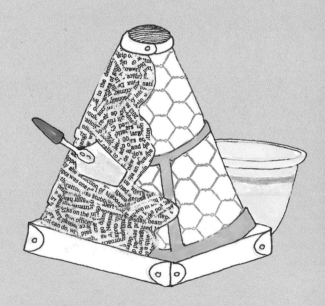